This is a book about two boys who are trying to escape. But each of them is running from a different thing.

"What are you running from?"

"They think I . . . "

Voices overheard in the dark. A beatup, stolen truck barrels down the highway. Then a match is struck in an abandoned cabin. The two boys look around. A map, a victrola, a gun.

This is a book about two boys trying to escape. One is pursued by love, the other by indifference. And neither of them gets away.

Escape *was first published in Czechoslovakia under the title* Útěk. *It won the Czech prize in an international contest for books for young people of the atomic age.*

ESCAPE

ESCAPE

BY OTA HOFMAN

ILLUSTRATED BY ALAN E. COBER

TRANSLATED BY ALICE BACKER

ALFRED A. KNOPF · NEW YORK

This is a Borzoi Book published by Alfred A. Knopf, Inc.
First American Edition
Copyright © 1970 by Alfred A. Knopf, Inc.
All rights reserved under International and Pan-American Copyright Conventions.
Published in New York by Alfred A. Knopf, Inc. and simultaneously in Toronto,
Canada, by Random House of Canada Limited.
Originally published in Czechoslovakia as ÚTÉK by Albatros, Prague.
Copyright © 1966 by Ota Hofman. Illustrations Copyright © 1970 by Alan E. Cober.
Library of Congress Catalog Card Number: 69-11546
Manufactured in the United States of America

ESCAPE

• BRONCO •

His nickname was Bronco. He whistled goodbye to his
friends, ran up the stairs, and rang the bell in the hall.
  "Hi, Mom."
He fell in, out of breath, and raced across the kitchen.
"Sasha!"
"What?"

He turned around. There were muddy footprints on the floor.

"What about your boots?"

He never could remember to take off his boots.

"You and that good-for-nothing Slip," said his mother.

He came back reluctantly, took off his boots one after the other, and wiped the mud from the linoleum.

"I'll go wash."

He went into the bathroom and turned on the shower.

"Don't forget to wash your ears," he heard from behind the door over the noise of the water.

"Yes, ma'am."

"And your feet."

"Okay."

He saw that there was a cigarette hole in his sweatshirt. He hid it in the hamper, down at the bottom. Then he pointed the shower nozzle at his plastic boat, which bounced back and forth in the tub. With his other hand he tried to soap the warpaint off his chest and stomach.

"Sasha!"

"Coming, Daddy."

He stepped into his shorts, at the same time pulling a box of matches from the pocket of his jeans. He hid them. Brushed his teeth for a whole minute with peppermint-flavored toothpaste and spit it out.

After that he opened the door.

No matter how careful he was, trouble usually caught up with him one way or another.

Breathe at me. Were you smoking?

"But I brushed my teeth," he thought.

What about the sweatshirt?

"They'll find that tomorrow. There'll be a lecture for sure," he told himself.

He closed the bathroom door and went into the livingroom in his bare feet. By the window the TV was on, but no one seemed to care about the floods in Italy or the arrival of the Czech cabinet ministers. His father was looking through his schoolbag. He had found the report card. Sasha realized he was going to get a lecture now.

Passed notes in class. Forgot compass and ruler. Caught with water pistol.

Those things had been signed last time.

Stuck gum to the desk.

That had not been signed.

"Why didn't you know your Latin?" his father asked.

"The Caesar part?"

His father read further; he became more serious.

Tripped a classmate. Shouted swear words.

Sasha began to defend himself. "It was Sally—she put leaves down my neck."

"And what did you swear?"

"Well . . ."

5

"What do you mean by swearing? Answer me."

His father raised his hand, but Sasha moved, just as on TV some racecars lined up for the start.

"I won't do it any more. I promise." There was a curve; one of the cars cracked up. "You'll see."

Slowly Sasha walked toward his father and picked up the schoolbag and the report card, which his father had signed angrily. He began to back out of the room, so he could see the screen for the finish. He stopped at the door.

"Can I stay?"

His father gave him a look. Sasha decided to back all the way out.

· SASHA ·

Beside his bed was a nightlight, which made him angry—he was not a baby. And the Latin.

He recited it for the tenth time.

A howling wind came through the walls of his bedroom, and rain was running down the window; it went rat-a-tat-tat on the sill.

Voices. Indians! A movie. They didn't let him watch television at night, but he could hear it and imagine.

Superman, walking through a solid wall.

No, this was a western. *High Noon*. The sheriff has been deserted by everyone, even the woman he loves.

Sasha forgot the poem.

Leaning on the pillow, he put his finger on the trigger and

began to fire as they came to get him.

Bang! Bang!

Ungh! Hit in the shoulder from ambush.

He rolled over and told Sally, who was watching help-lessly, "Nothing to it. I'll just tighten the bandage with my teeth. If only you hadn't yelled, it wouldn't have been on the report card."

He was dying . . . then he remembered the caps. They were in a tin can under a brick by the garage.

"If it keeps raining they'll be ruined. I'll have to get them first thing in the morning. I can't forget."

"And fill the fountain pen," he thought.

He pressed the button on his nightlight. He had to press it again and again in the exact center to turn it off, because the nightlight was so old.

"I want a regular lamp for my birthday," he thought.

The ceiling turned rosy in the darkness. Sasha lay with his eyes closed. He thought he heard shouts from the street. Then a window went up in the next room and someone went to the door. He could still hear the raindrops running down the window while in the distance there was the sound of sirens and fire engines. When he opened his eyes, the rain was the color of oranges!

Sasha jumped out of bed and walked through the empty apartment. Flames were billowing behind the hill in the distance.

In the corner the TV was still on—a boy in an old-fashioned coat from another century was walking through a graveyard as an eerie wind bent the treetops. Suddenly one of the trees

seemed to come to life and stretched its arm at the boy.

Sasha felt it on the back of his own neck. He shut his eyes.

• A MOUSE •

"I have a sore throat," he said the next morning so he wouldn't have to go to school.

"Did you know there was a fire last night?" asked his mother.

"Where?"

"That shed on the hill. At the housing project."

Two cups of tea with lemon. He drank them absent-mindedly. His mother took his temperature.

"There's nothing wrong with you."

She inspected his schoolbag in the hall. It had been a routine, of course, ever since they found the water pistol. He remembered the caps. "What about your pockets? Do you know your Latin?"

"Yes, Mom."

He went into the yard. Rainwater escaping through holes in the gutters was slapping the faded bricks of the garage. Sasha reached the gate. He could still go back, lift up the brick, and take out the tin can. He tried to imagine it. The rain dripping through the hole in the lid. The caps would be soaking wet. He wanted to go back, but no, he didn't.

It was seven-thirty in the morning in October, and the street was almost dark. The lights were still on in the dairy. He hoped to run into Summer and Slip.

Because it was *that* shed where they had been smoking yesterday. They had taken turns, one puff at a time.

"But we put it out," he thought.

He jumped a puddle and took a shortcut to wait for them at the underpass between the new apartments. He ran into some other boys from his class. Of course they were talking about it.

"I hear it was tar that caught fire."

"You going to look at it, Sasha?"

"Up there?" Sasha banged his schoolbag against a garbage can. "What for?"

But he followed them up the hill to the site of the fire. Yesterday there had been a shed with construction material, but now the girders stuck out like spikes. The roof had caved in and the grass was burned black. There were ruts from the tires of the fire engines. Partly burned shovels lay in the mud, and a large twisted screen.

Two women were coming down the path from the community gardens on the hill. One held a little child by the hand, the other a shopping bag. As they passed near Sasha, he heard them talking.

"Boys, probably."

"They were playing here yesterday."

He stepped out of their way. He was afraid someone might recognize him. "But we didn't do it, we didn't do it," he told himself over and over again. "It wasn't us."

The school came into view below him. The long lighted windows of the gym. It was a modern matchbox. Sasha walked down the hill with heavy feet. At the playground he saw Jokl and Exner bending over something on a schoolbag, something small and gray.

They caught sight of him.

"Hey, c'mere."

"It's still moving."

"A mouse!"

But Sasha kept on walking.

· SCHOOL ·

By the time Sasha reached his locker, he, too, had turned into something small. As he took off his coat, he also took off his Bronco self and hung it on the peg. He became Alexander, *Goosey Gander!*

There it was, written inside his sneakers in indelible ink, *Alexander Tichy, Grade Four.*

"Goosey Gander!"

Usually Sasha would fight when his schoolmates made fun of his name, but not now. Because he had just seen Summer. He followed him through a sea of girls and ribbons.

The school was new, it had just been built, but already it reeked of school as if it were a hundred years old. Nobody had asked for it; it had just come with the housing project. It replaced all the best forts and hideouts.

Summer pretended not to see Sasha. He was sweating, and the pimples on his nose shone. He motioned, "Beat it."

He was four years older than Sasha, in eighth grade.

He whispered under his breath, "The cops were at Slip's."

"When?"

"Never mind when. You weren't there yesterday, right?

Remember, *nobody was there*. Just keep quiet."

"Okay."

"So get off my back!"

Sasha left him alone. The bell rang. It was still raining. He walked down the hall past displays of weapons and the evolution of man. It was called a "school of the future." The classes watched television. Levers and lights all over. There was one class called "The Game of Numbers," where you stuck tiny cars and apples on a magnetic blackboard.

$$8 + 5 =$$

He went into his English class, where the teacher had projected the lesson on a movie screen:

Find misspelled words and write correctly:
His hair was dissheveled.
My uncle is a batcheler.
The forteenth rownd was a draw.
Fill in the blanks with ie *or* ei*:*
He did not bel ve his best fr nd would dec ve him.

The light blinked in front of him.

"Tichy."

Nobody was there.

It took him a minute to realize he had been called. He stood up, then bent down and rummaged frantically through his schoolbag for his notebook, afraid he had forgotten it, but he found it.

He sighed.

"Is something the matter?"

"No, ma'am."

He walked to the screen and pulled the lever. Fill in the blanks. The lever rapped along, *believe, deceive*.

"You see, you can do it when you want to."

Sasha looked up, startled. She had given him an A and put a gold star in his notebook.

He was happy for a second. Until a voice came over the intercom.

"Attention, Alexander Tichy of the fourth grade is to come immediately to . . ."

· T H E   L A W ·

"You know them?"

Summer and Slip were in the principal's office. Sasha started to shake his head ("Don't worry, I won't tell the cops"), but Slip nodded as if he should go ahead and tell, so in the end Sasha turned the motion into a nod. One of the two policemen had seen them.

"Look at *me*," he said. "How many cigarettes did you have?"

"Uh . . ."

Out of the corner of his eye Sasha saw Slip. He had three fingers hidden under the palm of his hand.

"Two," he said.

"No signaling."

"We're not signaling."

The other policeman looked fed up. "I don't need those first two any more," he snapped. "Maybe later." He waited until he was alone with Sasha.

"How did you get into the shed?"

"Along the board."

"Speak up," said the policeman. He was writing in a note-book. He looked up. "You were smoking in that shed and then Slip set the shavings on fire."

"But we put that out."

"How?"

"We just . . . just . . ." Sasha stammered. How to say it? "We watered it."

"All of you?"

"One after the other."

"What time was that?"

"About six."

"Then you went home?"

"Yes, sir."

"But Slip stayed behind in the shed."

"No, nobody did."

"Is that the truth?"

On the table was something wrapped in brown paper. Sasha couldn't tell what it was from where he stood, until the police-man lifted up the paper and pulled out a beer can. It was caked with dirt. Tiny snake-like roots grew from it. He shook a piece of paper out of the can. It had signatures on it.

"Know this?"

"Yes, sir."

It was their Secret Oath Written in Blood.

" 'One for all and all for one. Geronimo, Speed, Bronco.' You Bronco?"

"No."

"Yes you are. Sometimes they call you Goosey Gander

though. They make fun of you, you know. They only took you in so you'd get them cigarettes."

"That's not true!"

"Whatever you say."

The officer put the oath back in the can, and pushed the can under the wrapping paper. His hand felt for something else. The paper rustled as though a rabbit was under it.

"Who'd you leave behind in the shed, Summer or Slip?"

"Nobody."

"That's what you say."

It seemed to Sasha that the policeman was only sore because no one had stayed behind in the shed. The wrapping paper stopped rustling, and the policeman's hand reappeared. When he opened it, Sasha saw a dirty, half-burned bit of rag. It looked like part of a shirtsleeve, a checkered pattern of black, red, and yellow.

"What about this? Think. Which one of you was wearing a shirt like this yesterday?"

"Nobody."

"How do you know?"

"We wear sweatshirts. They're all alike."

"What kind?"

"Striped."

"Yesterday too?"

"Yes."

"All of you?"

Sasha thought. Then he said, absolutely honestly, "Yes."

But the policeman did not look satisfied. He put the burned sleeve back under the paper.

"You can go for now," he said. "But if you've lied to me——"

Everyone knew about it; the word had gotten around.

In the lunchroom the cook put dumplings on Sasha's plate and said to him, "Tell me what you did."

"Nothing."

She wouldn't believe him. "Don't try and fool me. It's plain as the nose on your face."

Sasha pulled his plate away and walked to a table. The lunchroom was half empty now.

He heard the dishwasher tell the cook, "They need a good spanking, those damn kids."

Sasha lost his appetite. Didn't know what he was eating. He stared blankly at the meat and cold tomato sauce lumped on his plate.

"I'm in for it," he thought, "even though nothing happened."

If you've lied to me——

He remembered the cigarettes. There had been eight; they had smoked four. There were four left in the box. If nobody was in around six, when Summer got home, he could have gone back to the shed. Or Slip. But Slip didn't have the matches, Sasha had the matches. By now they probably knew everything at home. They must have found the sweatshirt, even if it was at the bottom of the hamper.

He consoled himself, "But I got an A and a gold star in spelling."

Always the smell of something burning. He realized it was the tomato sauce and stopped eating. He felt sick to his stomach. Jumped when the door opened—he thought they were coming to get him again—but it was only some girls peeking in to look.

"That's him."

Jokl, who was sitting across from Sasha, had finished his lunch. He got up to wash his knife and fork. As he passed Sasha he said, "I bet they'll expel Slip."

"So what?"

Leaving the dumplings on the plate, Sasha followed Jokl to the recreation room. The pingpong table was taken. Two boys were kneeling on the floor painting a big poster, LONG LIVE LIBERATION DAY.

Sasha went to sit beside Jokl, and began to work on his Chinese lantern. "They can't expel him," he whispered. "Where would he go? Besides, we didn't do anything."

"Ha!"

Stupid Jokl.

The girls began to try out their lanterns, They lit candles from each other's, and Sasha went over and lit his, too.

He laughed at Jokl, "Beat it."

Sasha's lantern had a big crayon rocket and it was the most beautiful of all. The colored panels shone like stars.

"Save those lights for outside," said the teacher nervously, coming over and snuffing out Sasha's candle. "Want to set another fire?"

But the girls were allowed to keep theirs.

It was dusk. Chinese lanterns scattered in every direction, like fireflies. The sky was drizzling, and Sasha held his hand over his lantern to protect it from the rain. The last of the day's gravel trucks rumbled over the deep ruts in the muddy road of the housing project. He jumped aside to keep from getting splashed.

He stopped. Ahead of him was a blue car with a white stripe parked in front of his house.

"The police!"

All of a sudden his schoolbag weighed a ton. He hesitated, then quickly recrossed the street. A long line of people were waiting in front of the supermarket to buy oranges. On the volleyball field two men were jacking up a truck, pushing bricks under the frame.

He walked past them. They didn't even look up.

He could still see the street and the white stripe on the police car, but now he was high on the slope and from there the car looked like a toy. He kept walking. Scaled a pile of lumber. As he hid his lantern under one of the boards, he saw a girl from his class coming up the hill with a German shepherd.

The dog ran up to him and sniffed. It was a puppy and tried to lick his nose.

"Oof! Go sniff somewhere else!"

He threw a stone for the dog to chase, and turned to Sally. "You too," he growled.

Her feelings were hurt. She yelled back, "You'll be sorry, you just wait."

Sasha went around in circles.

For a while he walked above the railroad tracks, with their lit-up locomotives rushing back and forth, hissing steam. He was still in the city, but it was the night city, a Prague he didn't know, that frightened him, full of flashing neon and rectangles of light and smokestacks spitting fire into the darkness. It was raining and raining. The slope was soaked, and the mist made the clock by the tracks look like a full moon. Sasha took a cardboard clock from his schoolbag and set the hands.

He found some old cupcakes. Taking one, he ate as he walked, amid the screeching of locomotives, feeling beautifully sad.

"I'll never get back. I'll die. I bet they'd be glad to see me, too. They lock the door at nine. An hour left. And I got an A and a gold star. Besides, we didn't do it."

It was pouring now. The water ran down his neck and sloshed in his shoes from the puddles he walked through. The path zigzagged up the hill. He took a wrong turn once and had to go back, because the hill was different in the dark than in daytime. At last he bumped into the wire fence outside the community gardens. He walked along the fence, counting the metal poles.

One.

Five.

Eight.

He seemed to know every stone, for he squeezed through

some bushes and went straight to a hole in the fence. Squatting down, he wiggled through, schoolbag in front. A piece of wire caught him in the face.

All around, the gardens and gazebos were quiet. The arbors and toolsheds were so low he could touch the trellised tops and roofs. There were a thousand little fenced-off plots, with chrysanthemums blooming everywhere and the tree trunks painted white. Shining glass balls were fastened to the fence around his grandfather's plot.

Sasha put his hand through the wooden slats and felt for the latch on the gate. He closed it quietly behind him, and stood in the small courtyard. He knew the keys to the toolhouse were under one of the flowerpots by the doormat. He flipped over three pots before he found them. Then he gave a jump. The rumble of a motor came over the sound of the rain.

A car. Surprisingly, it came through the main gate, where there was a sign, PRIVATE PROPERTY. NO TRESPASSING.

Sasha groped at the keyhole. He unlocked the door, heart in his mouth as a searchlight swung over his head, stopped in the branches of a tree, then shifted.

The car came closer. It was blue with a white stripe.

Sasha leaned against the door and sighed with relief as he felt it give way.

Inside the toolhouse was a warm smell of rotting leaves and soil. He stood at the door in total darkness, afraid to move. He knew where he was, but the place was full of junk and he couldn't see it in the dark. A table, fruit trays, watering cans, garden tools, a rocking chair with a hole in the seat.

Gradually outlines emerged from the darkness. A thousand little hammers seemed to be rapping against the wooden walls of the shed, but it was only the rain and the crunch of tires on gravel.

A searchlight beamed under the eaves of the roof. The light went from corner to corner, and for a fraction of a second each one lit up. All of a sudden Sasha saw a white face against the opposite wall. He shrieked.

Then it was dark.

Images from the TV ran through his mind, of the treetops bending in the wind and the boy walking through the grave-yard. Now one of the trees came to life and stretched its arm at him. He felt it grip him by the neck.

• THE HAND •

Fingers. The smell of sweat.

A hand moved up and covered his mouth. "Shut up," he was told. "Quit yelling." It was a strange voice, almost plead-ing.

Sasha tried to bite the hand, and it withdrew. Something white hung from the wrist. A rag? A bandage?

Outside, the car picked up speed and seemed to come closer.

"If you've brought them here, I'll kick your teeth in," whispered the voice in the dark. It was shaking.

Sasha breathed, "No." He was trembling so much he could hardly speak.

The car moved rapidly away.

The stranger's hand still held him pinned down.

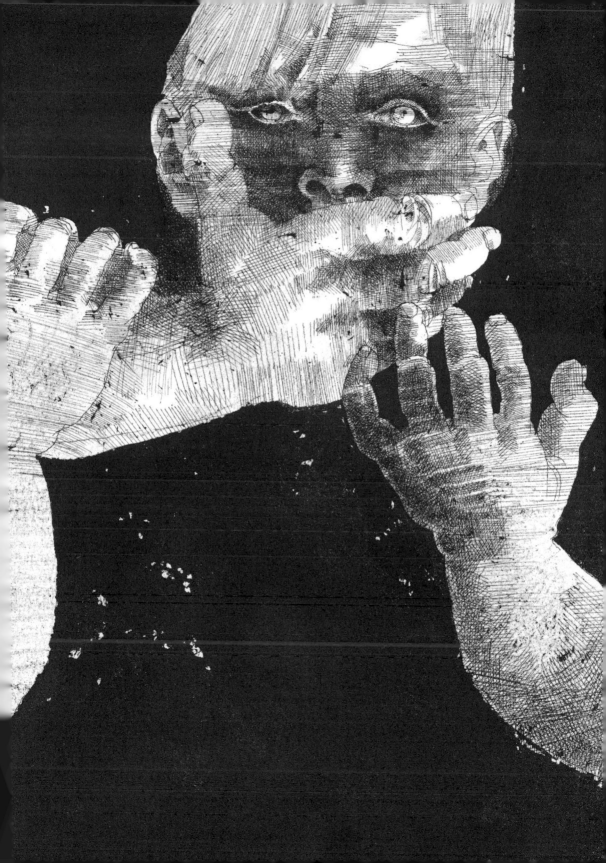

"They're probably looking for me," Sasha told him. He really thought so, but a moment later he realized that it was too early. They wouldn't look here right away. Not the police, anyway.

His captor seemed impressed by what he said, for he released his grip.

"Looking for you? What did *you* do?"

"Nothing."

"So why are they after you?"

"A couple of us——"

"Yeah?"

"They think we set the shed on fire."

"The one that burned down yesterday?"

"But all we did was smoke."

There was a whistle in the dark. The voice said, "Nice mess. You're in for it. How old are you anyway?"

"Almost ten."

"Oh yeah?"

A match struck. The stranger held it up for a minute and bent down to pick up the keys Sasha had dropped. His jacket fell open. Sasha saw that he was not wearing anything under it. No shirt. "What are you staring at?" he demanded.

Sasha remembered the checkered shirtsleeve the policeman had shown him. He stammered, "It must be cold like that—without a shirt."

"So what? Maybe I like it that way." The stranger zipped up his jacket and rattled the keys at Sasha's nose.

"This joint here—it belongs to your parents?"

"No."

"So where did you get the keys?"

"From under the flowerpot. They keep them there."

"How did ya know that?"

"It's Grandpa's. I come here to play. I have my toys here—in that crate."

"What toys?"

"Erectors and a crane. Two trucks." Sasha wanted to be believed. "And a hoe. And a shovel."

There was silence.

Whoever this was, he had probably looked everything over before anyway.

Sasha said, "Sometimes Grandpa comes here at night, too."

"Nah."

Sasha wished it was true. If only someone would come, even the police. Since now he knew who had set the shed on fire. He wasn't positive, but why would anyone go around in October like that, without a shirt?

Sasha said, "Slip had nothing to do with it."

The other one laughed. "Quit worrying. I'm not going to tell on you. I just came in for cover when it started to rain."

With that, he half-opened the door and looked out.

"Catch," he said, stepping into the little courtyard and throwing the keys at Sasha. They dropped on the doorsill. Sasha bent over and picked them up. He could hear footsteps on the gravel, and then the gate opened.

"Wait," he called, but the words stuck in his throat. Somehow he inserted the key, locked the door, and put the key back underneath the flowerpot. Then he ran out through the gate, calling after the retreating footsteps, "Wait, I have to tell you something——"

But he didn't know what it was. All he knew was that he

mustn't let the stranger get away. He ran down the path and tore through the bushes.

Terrified and yet thrilled.

He imagined telling Slip how he, singlehandedly . . .

• A KNIFE •

Sasha stumbled into the blackness. Then something heavy hit him and pushed him to the ground. He felt a sharp pain in his knee, and his mouth was full of dirt. He tried to spit it out, tried to get loose.

"Let go," he said. "Leggo! I'll tell. I'll be all muddy."

"Who cares?"

The weight shifted, and his opponent now sat on top of him. Sasha's schoolbag poked painfully into his stomach.

A streetlight swung back and forth across the fence, creaking in the wind. For a split second Sasha could see the face above him: it was a scared kid, with wet hair plastered to his forehead. Seventeen maybe. Maybe younger. The boy panted, "I'm not stupid, or maybe you think I am?"

"No."

But Sasha relaxed a little. It wasn't a horrible hand in the dark hanging over him any more. It was just an ordinary hand. It was a boy in a leather jacket who was sneering, "You want me to let you go, huh? So you can shoot your big mouth off."

"No."

"Yes—with that damned shed of yours. You'd let it all out. You're a rat—just like my brother."

The bandage on the boy's wrist was caked with mud.

Sasha pleaded, "No, I'm not like that."

"Shut up, for Chrissake." He renewed his pressure on Sasha and kept him pinned to the ground. They heard footsteps and voices on the walk outside the fence. "Who's that?"

Sasha listened and tried to guess. "The watchman."

"And who's that with him?"

A flashlight shone in the dark. It came along the fence in the direction of the little gate.

The watchman said, "Nobody there."

But the man with him walked ahead, saying, "We'd better take a look. He hasn't been home since morning. He never did that before."

The gate creaked. The watchman told him, "I told you it was locked. I bet he's home right now."

Sasha's companion hissed, "Oh boy, fathers!" and with an unmistakable motion snapped open a switchblade and held it under Sasha's nose.

Sasha sniffled. His eyes filled with tears.

When the two men had gone, the boy stuck the knife in the ground. "I was only kidding," he said. "What's the matter, can't you take a joke?"

He crawled ahead on his knees, then stopped and sniffed his hand. "Shit—cats everywhere!" Wiped his fingers on the grass.

He came to the hole in the fence. "You go first," he commanded, and turned to look at Sasha. "Don't think you can run out now. Not to send them after me."

They slid downhill, half running, tripping over clumps of weeds. They were both soaking wet. The older boy was rubbing his hand.

"You touch that stuff and you stink for a week!"

He said it to make the kid laugh. Then, "Say, he's okay."

"Who?"

"Your old man—looking for you."

Sasha was amazed—he couldn't imagine his father *not* looking for him. He started to cry, and wiped his nose on his sleeve.

"Hold it," said the older boy, "you're making a mess of yourself." He spit in his handkerchief and wiped off Sasha's nose with it. They walked on for a few minutes.

"Say, you always cry like that?"

Sasha limped behind. He shook his head and sniffled, "I left my schoolbag there."

They went back and found it lying in the grass.

The big boy picked it up. "Jesus, it weighs a ton." He swung it around. "All that smarty-pants school stuff. Hah! Tell me: if there's ten sparrows sitting on a roof and I shoot one, how many are left?"

"None," Sasha said without a moment's pause. "That junk's even in our reader. Wait, I'll show you." He took the bag and rummaged through it. Pulled out a book. "They're just stupid tricks."

"Okay, that'll do." Something else had caught the boy's eye. There was wax paper in the bag. Without a word he pulled it out and unwrapped the leftover cupcakes. Through his munching could be heard, "Give my regards to your mother."

It made Sasha hungry just to look at him.

The other boy noticed it at about the last bite. "Want some?"

He divided the rest.

"Thanks," Sasha said mechanically. It was his own cupcake.

The older boy licked the paper. "I could sure use a cigarette," he said.

Sasha thought a minute, then ran a few steps down the hill and pointed. "There's a cigarette machine down there."

"Where?"

"By the phone booth. But you have to put in a crown."

The boy looked uncertain. He felt in his pocket and came up with a handful of coins, five crowns or so in small change. He peered down the hill in the direction Sasha was pointing. "There's only a newspaper stand," he said suspiciously.

"And a cigarette machine. And a phone booth. They put them up at least a year ago. Over by that wall."

• THE NIGHT BUS •

Sasha followed him down the hill.

They stopped at a small lot where some cars were parked under awnings. Trucks too.

"Nothing here," said the older boy, suspicious again. He rapped the fenders of the cars. Every so often he tried a door. "So where's the cigarette machine?"

"Around the corner."

Sasha led the way now. He was hoping against hope to run into someone, but the street was deserted. They passed a police alarm box. Some people were waiting at a bus stop ahead of them. A man and a woman walked out of one of the houses. The night bus was coming. Sasha gathered up his courage and ran after them.

"Please!"

But they were hurrying to catch the bus. "It's quarter to ten," called the man helpfully. They got on the bus.

The boy caught up with Sasha. He grabbed his schoolbag, and then his coat, not gently, either. "It's that late, is it? Boy, we'll get it at home!" Loud enough to make the man hear.

Sasha gasped. The way he lied! He was really a liar. He tried to wiggle free.

No use.

"Next time you'll be glad you're in one piece," said the boy. "Go on!" He squeezed Sasha's arm and opened the door to the phone booth with the same motion. "Crawl," he said, shoving Sasha in with his knee.

A few people who had got off the bus walked by.

"But the cigarette machine is really there, cross my heart," cried Sasha, terrified. "There!"

Twenty feet from the phone booth the cigarette machine was standing against the wall.

"If you want me to——"

The boy ignored him. He dug in his pocket and found a piece of paper. Dialed.

A man's voice answered.

"It's me," the boy said. "Who am I? Don't you know? I'm the sucker who didn't squeal on you." He laughed, then said,

"What do *you* think? Maybe they *let* me go."

There was a click at the other end. He dialed the number again. Busy. "Okay, Little Bo Peep."

He turned to Sasha and indicated the cigarette machine. The street was empty. Then he reached in his pocket and brought out another piece of paper and dialed another number.

"Hello?" It was a woman's voice.

"Is Alice there?" He wet his lips as he waited. There was a long silence.

"Who's calling?" said the woman. When the boy did not answer, she said, "She's gone for the weekend. Who is this?"

He hung up. He felt in his pocket and found four crowns. Shoved them at Sasha. "Filters."

Sasha went out, turning around once to look back at the booth. He crossed the street and looked back again. Then he stood on tiptoe at the machine and put the money in.

He clutched the cigarettes in his hand and started to run back.

But he had to slow down. There was a car passing, a convertible. By the time he reached the booth it was empty.

• THE TRUCK •

He climbed back up the hill. He was furious with himself, swearing, "If it had been Slip, he'd never have let him get away." He crawled through the bushes and snorted. "Dumbhead!"

Below him a car door slammed shut with a tinny sound.

Then another one. Someone was going from car to car. A starter broke the silence. The noise reverberated off the sleeping houses.

Sasha went limp. He took a hesitant step downhill and stopped. Another two steps and he slid down the slope. He heard a motor running; the sound came crazily close. He waited at the edge of the lot as a truck approached.

Suddenly he caught sight of a handhold and grabbed on, somersaulting up into the back of the truck just as it turned the corner. He landed on a pile of damp sand and was tossed here and there, his cheek now on the schoolbag, now in the sand. Flickering lights swam past.

Bumps and more bumps shook the truck whenever the driver shifted gear. The road was somewhere underneath, but all Sasha could see were the streetlights on high poles above him. Now and then the truck rattled over a hole; he could feel the asphalt change to cobblestone and back to asphalt. The top of a streetcar went by. Sparks flew from the electric line, then it was dark.

He managed to pull himself to a standing position at the side of the truck and leaned on a piece of bent metal. His arms ached. Behind him in the distance was a glow. The lights of the city were receding. Prague was vanishing.

He dozed in fits and starts. Now the truck rumbled through the main street of a small town, and he awoke abruptly, with one cheek buried in the wet sand. He did not know how long he had been asleep—maybe five minutes, he guessed. Lights flitted in between the boards on the side of the truck: they were passing a car.

He stood up, but only for a second. His right leg hurt and

his teeth were chattering. He rubbed his knee. He wanted to go home, he was tired, he wished none of this was happening. To be able to wake up in his own bed and have the hated nightlight over his head—Sasha almost cried at the thought.

The headlights of the truck licked the milestones and the branches of trees—one tree, eight, a hundred, a thousand trees. A strange world of light and sound flew by: white trees, music from a merry-go-round at a picnic grounds, an old-fashioned water pump at a crossing, a train.

Off and on he had crazy dreams: Summer was on his bike, trying to catch the truck, reaching for it with his hand. Slip hung from a train, shouting, "We've got him surrounded. All for one and one for all!"

A jolt threw Sasha across the floor of the truck. It was quiet. They had stopped in the middle of nowhere.

· N I G H T ·

It was dark all around. The headlights shone on some bushes at the edge of a forest. The water in the radiator was boiling over.

Sasha heard the cab door click open in front, and then someone jumped down onto the road. He recognized the jacket: for a second it gleamed in the headlights, then it went off through the bushes and disappeared in the darkness.

He was afraid of being left alone with the night, which was all around. As he crawled quietly to the end of the truck, there was a tinny click, a thump.

The driver turned cautiously in the direction of the noise. For a moment he thought he wasn't hearing right. Maybe it was the engine cooling. The sound of the radiator boiling came across clearly in the silence.

Then another rustle from the back of the truck. Something dropped to the ground and lay motionless under the taillights. The driver didn't know what it was yet, but he was ready to run for it. Only no, he realized that was silly when he saw who was under the taillights, inching awkwardly across the ground, picking up his schoolbag, crawling slowly to the ditch. He stopped, then started again.

The older boy watched with amusement. Calmly he finished relieving himself, then with his back to Sasha, said, "So it's you again."

He turned, zipping up his fly. "I don't like being watched——"

"But I, I didn't mean . . ."

"I'm going to leave you here," he said. He jumped over the ditch and walked toward the truck. "And the hyenas are going to eat you alive."

He started the motor and the truck jerked forward. In the rearview mirror he could see the kid running after him as he drove away.

"Mister . . ."

The taillights blinded Sasha. He ran on for a moment longer, then gave up and stood still.

Looking in the mirror again, the boy saw Sasha scrawl something in the sand at the side of the highway, just as a glow rose over the hill from the opposite direction. He slammed on the brakes and jumped out, leaving the motor running.

He ran back, shouting, "Where the hell are you?"

The truck's license number had been written in the sand. He wiped it out furiously. A bird flew up. He heard the sound of feet running across the road, and chased after them.

"Real smart," he said, grabbing Sasha, who squirmed like a rabbit. "I get the picture now, you brat!"

Headlights swung over the top of the hill.

"Just what do you think you're doing?"

When Sasha didn't answer, the boy slapped him. "What do you think you're doing?"

"I'm going to stop a car." Sasha's lip was bleeding and he licked it. "I want to go home. Lemme go. I'll hitchike."

The headlights came closer.

"Let go!"

Sasha fought back, dragging his feet as the boy pulled him toward the truck, then picked him up and heaved him into the cab.

"So you want to go home, huh?" He squeezed in over Sasha's knees. "That's good. Run to Mama."

The truck moved into the headlights of an oncoming milk wagon.

"And now would you please shut your trap?" He was out of breath and sweating. "I hope you know we're in this together now."

They were on the highway again. Sasha couldn't see over the dashboard. "I want to go home!"

"Shut up, will you?"

He was concentrating on driving. He shifted into third gear. It was rolling countryside all around.

"I could have left you there. I would have been far away by now."

"No, you were afraid——"

"Afraid of what?" Suddenly he remembered: "What about my cigarettes? I gave you four crowns."

Sasha pulled the crumpled pack from his pocket, and it was snatched away.

"Why should I be afraid?"

"Because you burned down that shed," Sasha said.

"What makes you think so?"

"I know, because I saw the shirt."

"I didn't mean to." He took a cigarette and began to roll it back into shape. "Couldn't you have mangled them some more?"

He lit the cigarette with matches from the dashboard.

"I was drying my shirt, that's all," he said. "I fell asleep. You should have seen it. Wow!" He laughed and looked down. "Anything else you'd like to know?"

"Is this your truck?"

No answer. He smoked and looked ahead at the road.

"Then you stole it." Sasha's voice was serious.

They went up another hill. In the distance a stoplight was blinking like a firefly.

Sasha sniffled. It was cold in the cab.

The boy handed him a blanket from the back of the seat. "Go on, put it over you."

There was a pause.

"Well, I'll tell you. It's *our* truck now. Well, almost," he said, breathing on his fingers to warm them. "If you keep a thing, see, you're stealing it. But we won't keep it. We'll just ride in it for a while. Stealing—that's if you swipe a thing and put it in your pocket."

He drove with one hand on the wheel. "If you want to know, I think you're lucky. At least you're going someplace, seeing something."

"Going where?"

"Wherever we feel like."

But he didn't finish. There was a car ahead, a Skoda. He put out his cigarette and gripped the wheel with both hands.

"Watch this!"

The truck accelerated. He flicked the lights on and off, trying to get the Skoda to pull over. No use, it hugged the middle of the road like a turtle.

"Come on, you!"

Then a shout from the Skoda. "Hey you guys, who do you think you are—Mario Andretti?"

"So I'm 'Mario,' am I? All right, I'll show them how a real racedriver does it. Here we go!"

The truck went over the hill hard on the Skoda. A curve.

"Mario" slammed on the brakes and turned pale. "Damned curve!" he swore.

The truck skidded downhill, but in control. Coming into view in the headlights was a squat car with a broad white stripe. It was parked at the side of the highway. A red light was flashing.

Still in front of them, the Skoda pulled over.

• A CONVOY •

"If you so much as open your trap!"

Mario looked smaller, seemed to have lost pounds in the few minutes it took them to come up even with the police car. A flashlight was scanning the license of the Skoda. A highway patrolman looked up—he could be seen very clearly in the glare of the headlights—and waved them on.

Mario could hardly believe his eyes. He did not understand until he had passed the police car and saw a convoy of trucks coming up behind them in the rearview mirror. Lights were blinking, horns honking. The convoy passed the truck. There was machinery swaying under the canvas.

"Ha!" he exulted. "They thought this truck was part of the convoy!" He laughed and licked his lips. "What a break. Jesus!"

He looked for the cigarettes and matches.

"Light me one," he said, pushing the cigarettes at Sasha. "C'mon, do what I say."

Now he concentrated on keeping the truck within three yards of the taillights of the convoy truck just ahead.

But Sasha was angry. The older boy was whistling and he couldn't bear it. Spitefully he crushed the cigarette in his hand before he lit it. Smoke stung his eyes and throat. He began to cough.

38

"Want one?" said Mario drily. He took the lighted cigarette and offered Sasha the pack. "Go on, take one if you want."

Sasha shook his head doggedly.

Laughter. "Well, you can't say I didn't —"

"But I will say—everything!"

"Okay, okay, but save it for later. First we'll go for a ride." For a second the glow of the cigarette lit Mario's face, which was weary. "Ever see an iguana with two humps?"

"An iguana. What's that?"

"A kind of pig with wings. Africa is full of them," said Mario knowingly.

The motor hummed, the dashboard blinked. Sasha could imagine the truck going all the way to Africa. "But it's lions that live in Africa."

"Yeah, lions too. And turtles and alligators and lots of all kinds of wild animals. The best."

"But I have school tomorrow."

Sasha's words seemed to come from very far away. Through half-closed eyes he watched in a daze as the older boy tightened the bandage on his wrist with his teeth.

"Anyway, I'm going to tell. No matter what," he murmured.

A hand stopped the blanket from sliding off. Mario slowed down. The needle indicated that they were almost out of gas—barely a third of a tank left.

"Sleep," he said. "I'll wake you up when we get there."

Fog covered the windshield.

The fog was thicker near the riverbank. On the highway the dump truck came out of the white steam as though from a laundry. Mario drove it off onto a gravel side road. The pebbles crunched under the tires and rattled against the sides. For a while there was nothing but fog, the sound of the gravel, and the revolutions of the engine.

Dawn lit the sky.

They were out of sight of the highway. The truck coasted a few yards farther and stopped. Sasha was asleep, and not even the jerk of the brakes awoke him.

The gas needle was on Empty. Very quietly Mario checked the glove compartment. He took some keys and two screwdrivers, opened the door, and jumped onto the grass. Sizing up the vicinity, he saw that there was an overpass that would screen the truck from above, and on both sides were trees.

It could have been worse. It would probably be two hours before the truck was discovered.

He put the screwdrivers and keys in his pocket, and began to walk along a path that followed the river, then veered up a hill toward some woods. He walked briskly, stopping to dip his hand in the water and splash his face. He wanted to go to sleep but was afraid to risk taking the time—they might find the truck, they might have dogs on him.

His sandals were wet. Leaves stuck to them. Dew glistened on the sharp blades of grass.

He froze at the sound of breaking twigs. Footsteps. Slowly he turned to look behind him.

Someone called sleepily, "Where are they?"

He saw the boy running after him, schoolbag in hand, dragging the blanket, which had slipped from his shoulders.

"Where are they?"

"What?"

"The iguanas?"

It took him a minute to remember Africa. Birches all around, masses of leaves. "We're not quite there yet," he said. "Go on back to the truck and go to sleep. I'll come for you. What's the matter, don't you believe me?"

Sasha shook his head and followed like a dog. Picking up a branch and striking trees with it, he said out of nowhere, "They're going to expel Slip."

"So what?"

"Because of the shed."

So it wasn't Africa. The kid wasn't that dumb after all. Mario stopped a yard ahead of him. He was getting mad. "You and your shed!" He had lost minutes of his headstart. Iguanas! "Beat it! Go back to the truck and stay there. Or do you want me to hit you?"

He resumed climbing but behind him the sniffling continued. It was like a whole kindergarten following.

"Didn't you hear me?"

Sasha had heard, but he knew that to stay behind meant he would never see the other boy again. He stumbled forward, feet slipping. He grabbed at bushes, at grass, out of breath from trying to keep up. The schoolbag was heavy.

He called, "Mister——"

The older boy stopped and waited. Sasha froze. He had a revolver in his hand.

"I——"

He raised the revolver.

Sasha fell back one step, two, then slipped on the wet roots and tumbled down the slope, rolling in the leaves. The trees went around in circles.

· TOGETHER ·

There was a dirt road leading up the hill, but Mario did not take it. Instead, he walked through the woods on a diagonal. The trees seemed endless. Another wooded hillside was visible through a clearing, and another beyond that. The peeled trunks of the pines looked red in the morning sunlight.

The woods were quiet and wet. Now and then the ground gave way; he sidestepped a bog. He tripped on a root buried under dead leaves and fell, striking something hard in his pocket. He pulled out his transistor radio to see if it still worked. There were a few things he really cared about, and the transistor was one of them.

Holding the radio up to his ear, he turned the knob. A tiny electric hum reassured him. He turned up the volume, and the sound of an electric guitar ripped through the forest like the cry of some strange animal. Then silence.

Suddenly the bushes rustled. Sasha appeared at the edge of the clearing, all covered with leaves, nose dripping.

"Wait for me," he panted.

He had been more afraid of the dark than of anything else. He looked over his shoulder. "I got scared back there all by myself."

Mario said nothing, didn't even chase him off. Here, near a road, it was too risky.

"Better take him with me," he thought. "I can always get rid of him when I want to."

• A R R O W S •

They had been walking for some time, at a distance from each other and mostly in silence. Sasha limped slightly. His boots were tight.

He sniffled, "My feet hurt."

He was trying to get attention. He dragged his right foot for a while. Then, as if idly, the toe of his boot drew an arrow pointing in the direction they were walking.

It might have been the tenth such arrow. The first one was near the truck by the river. Sasha hoped the police would find them—and the notebook he had left in the truck.

He said, "Maybe it's because I haven't eaten . . ."

Mario did not answer. He was scanning a row of bungalows that lay ahead of them on the slope. He ran up to one, then came back.

He lit a cigarette, coughed, and spat. "You and your god-damn shed!" Then, "What's your name?"

"Alexander."

Mario shook his head. "I don't envy you that one," he said. "There should be a law against dumb names."

He barely had time to finish. He pulled Sasha down into the underbrush.

Some horses came out of the trees like huge phantoms.

Steam poured from their nostrils, their harnesses rattled. There was a man leading them who was talking to himself out loud. The animals passed close to the two boys, grotesquely enlarged as seen from below, with enormous bellies swaying from side to side and blotting out the sky. Their hooves spattered mud.

Mario could feel Sasha trembling next to him. He said contemptuously, "Horses. As if you'd never seen a horse."

"Not so big. Littler."

"Ponies?"

"No, big horses, but not this big. If they run off the road we're goners."

But the horses dissolved in the fog as though they had never existed.

Mario got to his feet. He sucked on a blade of grass. "Horses are smarter than people. They wouldn't hurt you."

"No?"

"No. Well, of course if they went crazy——"

"Then they might?"

"Sure they might."

They trudged ahead, with the branches raining water on them. Mario was almost asleep on his feet.

Sasha kept two paces behind him. He thought about horses going crazy and about Mario. Where did he come from? Why was he running away?

Where was he going?

Quite unexpectedly they came on a row of log cabins in the middle of the woods. The one nearest them was black, with a sloping tarpaper roof painted red, and a chimney. The porch steps had been cut into the hill and were overgrown with grass. All the windows were shuttered, and the logs glistened with resin and tar.

Mario tried the door. It was locked. "We're home," he said.

He inspected the lock. There were two screws at the top, two at the bottom. He figured that the catch must be inside. He took some wire and one of the screwdrivers from his pocket.

"Go get some water. Go on," he told Sasha. "That flagstone path probably leads to water. And walk on the stones. No footprints."

There was a battered bucket under the porch, shot full of holes. Sasha took it.

At the spring a frog was sitting on a leaf. Sasha chased it away into the grass, and threw his schoolbag at it. He scooped up some water and stepped back over the schoolbag. "I'll leave it here," he decided. "If only he doesn't remember. Ten arrows, the notebook in the truck, and the schoolbag here— they can't miss them all."

He held the bucket half a yard from his leg to keep it from splashing on his feet. When he reached the cabin the door was open.

The walls smelled like oak. A candle caught flame, and went out again—the wick was wet. Mario struck his third match, and finally lit it.

In the dusky light the trembling flame reminded Sasha of the tree lights that flickered behind the windows of Prague at Christmas.

But the windows here were shuttered. Ordinary things looked frightening in the dark. The edges of the cupboards and the arms of the chairs seemed to strike out at him. The floor creaked at every step.

On the mantel was a shiny ceramic statue. Mario held the candle up. "Look here. A fish with ears." He laughed, but as if he were forcing it.

He walked across the room. He had unearthed a box of crackers somewhere, and threw it on the table in front of Sasha.

"Eat!" But the crackers crumbled into pieces.

A strange ceiling leapt into view as Mario picked up the candle and went to the door. Someone's book was lying open on the table.

Mario poured some of the water from the bucket into a jar, and splashed the rest over their footprints on the porch. He closed and bolted the door. Something tingled for a second, then the lock clicked shut.

"Neat," he said.

He bent over the candle and lit the butt of his last cigarette. His hands were shaking. "When they come to get us, they'll find us in a strongbox."

"Who?"

"The iguanas."

Mario coughed. He took a fistful of crackers and poured some water in a cup to wash them down.

"Want some?"

He poured water for Sasha. "I'd make a fire," he said, "but they might see the smoke. Otherwise we could have hot tea." He drank the water, and the crackers lumped in his mouth. He scowled at the mantelpiece, then at the yellowing pictures of racehorses and greyhounds hanging on the walls.

"Some nut," he said. "Fish with ears and moldy crackers. Never ate anything so revolting." He grimaced as he chewed. "Aren't they moldy?"

"Yeah, moldy."

But they ate them.

"Give me some plain old hot tea," Mario said, "gallons of tea. You should've stayed behind in the truck. They'd have found you by now."

"What time is it?"

"Going on nine."

Sasha was brushing crumbs from his coat collar by the light of the candle. The velvet was wet and matted. "Math at nine," he said out loud.

He started. A kind of shriek had come from outside.

Through a gap in the shutters they could see the opposite hill and even beyond. Axes were ringing. The crown of a tall pine shivered, then the tree fell. Several men were standing in a clearing in the distance.

"Felling trees," Sasha said in awe. He had never seen a live tree fall. "It's like it's dying, like in the movies."

48

Mario was silent. He turned his back. He had noticed a wickerwork dartboard and arrows on the wall, and shot for the bull's-eye a few times.

"Another tree's ready to fall," called Sasha. "Don't you want to see it?"

"No."

Mario opened the door to a closet. Inside were blankets, and an old sweater and giant-size pair of pants. He threw the sweater and pants to Sasha. "Bundle up or you'll catch cold."

As for himself, he put a straw hat on his head and draped a checked blanket over his shoulders like a poncho. He moved toward the stairs, then came back for the candle.

By the time Sasha had pulled the sweater over his head, the room was nearly pitch dark. Shadows were everywhere; he could feel his heart beating.

He ran to the stairs: "Mister!"

"Quit yelling."

The candle stopped. On the stairs Mario turned around to look at Sasha standing below him. He began to laugh aloud.

"You're a funny man," he said. With sweater sleeves a foot too long and wide pants folding around his boots, the boy looked like Charlie Chaplin. "Wanna see something, you comic strip?"

The candle was flickering over part of an upstairs room and an attic. In the steep roof a little window let light in on a discarded baby carriage and what looked like a lot of old junk. Mario began to climb up the ladder to see. He whistled through his teeth. "Alexander?"

He was exploring the trash in the attic. "Want some water goggles? A harpoon?" He turned around and put the goggles

on Sasha. One lens was missing. "How about an abacus?"
He squeezed over to the little window to get the abacus, and
knocked it down with his elbow. The beads jingled.

He stopped. Through the dirty window he could see down
the flagstone path to the spring. There was the schoolbag lying
in the grass.

· THE STAIRCASE ·

Sasha wanted to run, but there was nowhere to run to. The
door clicked downstairs. Silence. Then another click. Sasha
stopped halfway down the stairs.

Mario walked into the cabin, schoolbag in hand. He was
pale; drops of sweat showed on his nose. He came up to Sasha
and began to beat him with the bag, on the head, on the arms,
from all sides, as the boy backed up the stairs tripping, hid-
ing his face with his elbow. The strange thing was that it
happened in silence, with only an occasional sob or banging
sound in the dusk. Sasha tripped again and fell. Then it was
dark.

· THE MAP ·

He lay on a bed, the schoolbag next to him. He hurt all over.
He felt his face for a minute: the skin was burning. An ax rang
somewhere. Nothing around him looked familiar. He thought
he was alone.

He began to cry. "They'll never find me." He tried to guess

what time it was. "Math at nine. History." He sat up awkwardly and got to his feet.

Through the open door he saw Mario in the next room, standing under the eaves. A victrola with an old-fashioned trumpet stood in one corner of the room, and a black umbrella hung underneath the window. There was a desk with a bowl of pipes on it.

Sasha was afraid Mario would beat him up again, but strangely he didn't care. He was more afraid of being left alone. He shuffled to the door.

Mario opened a drawer and took out a box of Havana cigars. Under it he discovered a can of lighter fluid. He turned around.

"You never saw anything like it," he said to Sasha as though nothing had happened. He held up a little rocket that was mounted on a spring. When he pressed the spring the rocket shot up. "A pencil sharpener!"

He spoke as though he had made it himself.

"Wanna try it?"

But Sasha did not move. He was looking at the table with the revolver lying on it.

Mario seemed completely oblivious. He opened the barrel of the revolver and dripped lighter fluid on the cotton wool inside. Then he pulled the trigger and watched the flame contentedly. It was a cigarette lighter!

Sasha awoke from his trance. "I thought——"

Mario clicked the trigger once more. "You thought what?"

Then he understood.

"Are you crazy?" Mario said. "A gag—see? Would you shoot anybody?"

"No."

"Okay, so you see."

He let Sasha pull the trigger. Not a word about what had gone on before.

He rolled a cigar between his fingers. "I wouldn't even care about that shed," he said oddly, "except that I bungled something, something else before."

"What?"

"Nothing."

He was on his guard again, as if he were sorry he had mentioned it. He lit the cigar. "It wouldn't be so bad to have a cabin like this. What do you think?" He turned around and noticed an old map hanging on the wall.

"Hey—Africa!"

• HUNGER •

The axes were still ringing. They searched the cabin inch by inch, dragging striped socks and vests out of drawers, looking for something to eat. Mario discovered a crate in one corner of the kitchen. It took him half an hour to pry it open, only to find it full of old books and bound magazine volumes.

On the pages of a German edition of Brehm's *Natural History* were pictures of bats and leaping monkeys. For a minute Sasha forgot everything else; he looked at the pictures.

"Want to see a zebra?" he asked Mario.

"I wouldn't mind a zebra steak."

"Phoo."

"You'd lick your chops, I bet."

Mario crawled down into the cellar. There were a number of empty bottles lying on the floor, and he raked through them and found three bottles of wine and two cans. He held the candle up to the labels of the cans: paint.

"Delicious. Zebra steak with paint."

He climbed back upstairs with the bottles. Cheap red wine. "If worse comes to worst, we could get drunk. Why don't you take a nap and dream about sauerbraten in cream sauce?"

Sasha was kneeling in front of a small cabinet in the hall. He was pulling things out of it. A rod and reel. A box of glittering flies. Flies and hooks. He said excitedly, "Here's something." He held up a long cylindrical can, and watched tensely as Mario came up to him.

"Probably frankfurters," said Sasha. "The label's in English." He began to read it out loud: "Three balls, super." There was a key soldered to the bottom of the can. He broke it off.

Mario said, "I'll give you a crown if you eat them."

The can opened with a hiss of air.

Mario took it from Sasha and peeled off the lid. He emptied the contents on the floor.

"Shit," said Sasha, watching the tennis balls bounce across the room. "Three balls super. Shit!"

He barely noticed when Mario corrected him with a grin, "One doesn't say 'shit.' "

"Okay." But he added, "Ratfinks. Stuffing tennis balls in a tin can!"

They had nine crackers left. Sasha was lying on the bed, watching Mario's hand. It stacked the crackers in two even piles. The last cracker was an odd one. Mario hesitated, then broke it in two and gave half to Sasha and put the rest in his mouth. He munched slowly to make it last.

Mario poured himself some wine. "I'll leave the water to you," he said magnanimously. "Don't drink it all at once. We won't be able to leave before dark."

"Spiders in here," Sasha said. He lay on his back and looked at a spider web on the ceiling.

"So what?"

Mario felt too lazy to talk. For a while he observed the hair on the back of his hand. It was red. Light came in between the logs, that and the sound of the saw.

"Spiders are everywhere," he said indifferently, and sipped the wine. "In the woods and here and in Prague. Once we found a whole nest in the workshop."

"They have nests?" said Sasha.

"Some do and some don't." He didn't know exactly. "These here probably don't." He looked at the web. "In South America they're big as your thumb. They bite you and pffft— funeral. In South America, somewhere around there."

"Tarantulas?"

"Probably."

A second later he said, "How did you know that?"

"I read stuff like that. With my father."

"What stuff?"

"About astronauts and nature." Sasha hesitated a minute,

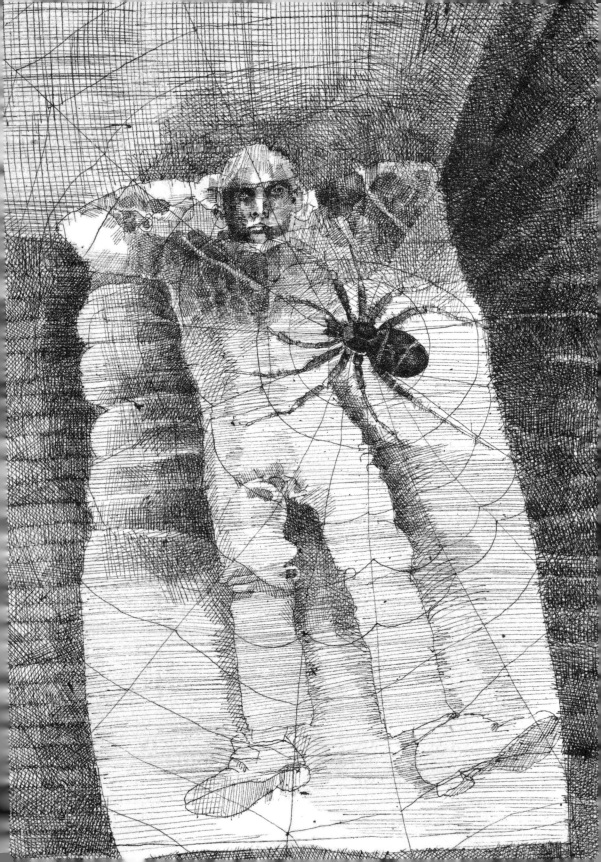

not sure whether he should tell. "I'll probably be an astronaut," he said.

"Or a ditchdigger," said Mario.

"Why a ditchdigger?"

"As if they didn't have enough ditchdiggers to go around, you dummy, did anybody ask you?" His voice rose. Then, seeing the kid's eyes, he added, "Maybe they will ask you. If you get straight A's."

"Two B's."

"What?"

"It's worse," said Sasha, who hated to repeat unpleasant things.

"I see."

Mario lost interest. He lay there yawning and looking through the edge of the shutter at the hill beyond. Sniffling and the crunching of crackers broke the silence. He couldn't stand it. Rolled over on his stomach.

"Maybe you should study more."

"That's not it."

"What is, then?"

"Once you get a noose, you've got it forever."

"What's a noose?"

"A flunk, an F."

"Maybe not," said Mario indecisively. "Maybe not forever." But he did know that some things stick like glue. They dog you even when everyone says it's forgotten. You never get rid of them. "Maybe not forever," he repeated. "One day everything is bound to change."

He wished he knew when.

"I'm counting on going into the military. If I can get into the auto corps. Jeeps, tanks, or ground air force."

The woodsmen were still on the hill. A tall tree was visible through the shutter. It shuddered and fell.

"What time is it?"

"Going on two."

Mario looked at Sasha. "Try to get some sleep," he said. "We have a long way to go. Your feet will hurt." He reached for another cracker and crumbled it into the wine. "I have money someplace. We can buy whatever we want then."

"Bread?"

"Yeah, bread and salami and pickles. Beer and lemonade—everything."

He lay on the bed with his eyes open, and looked at the ceiling and the spider's web, and at a picture that hung on the wall. It was a maze of black lines on a white background. There was a beetle crawling up the frame. It came to the edge and stopped. Mario watched it, then reached for a stick and knocked it off.

The beetle fell, then began to climb back up.

· MARIO ·

He was afraid of being alone too, yet he knew that he would always be alone, just as he had known from the beginning that escape was impossible. From nothing to noplace. Sometimes he tried to make himself believe that somebody was waiting for him, caring about him, but he knew no one was.

They would be scared of him, now that they knew he had run away. That phone call was the first mistake. He should have taken them by surprise. Taken the money and run. Fifteen hundred, for which he had been making his bed in reform school for two years.

It occurred to him, "I don't even know what Alice looks like now. I'm running because of somebody without a face. No, that's not true. I'm not running for anybody. I'm living and breathing. I feel great. This escape is a present from me to myself, like the transistor for Christmas. I'm lying in bed and nobody is yelling at me. I feel great. This cabin and the wine and the brat with his nooses and tennis balls in a tin. Everything."

He longed to live like this always.

"I'll take the brat and go to work in the forest and catch rabbits."

He decided to tell Sasha that. He groped up and down the next bed for a minute, but it was empty.

· A SAILBOAT ·

Sasha was in the other room, kneeling on a chair in front of the wall map. He was measuring the distance between Europe and Africa with his fingers. Five fingers wide.

He looked over his shoulder. "It's only a little way," he said sheepishly. "There, Afri-KA. Do you pronounce it Afri-KA?"

Quickly Mario covered the part of the map Sasha had measured with his hand. "This is the ocean," he said.

The ocean was blue like the sky. No bridges anywhere, and waves rolling in. He saw two very disappointed eyes.

"I thought," said Sasha, "that we could look it over for a while. Then we could come back. We could send a postcard from there to school, tell them how it was with that shed and that we'll bring them a live chimpanzee. Or a parrot. Or whatever we caught."

Mario didn't answer. He knew there was no point in saying anything, at least not now. "Hey—a record player," he exclaimed, as though they had been talking about record players the whole time.

He walked to the victrola, picked up the needle, and tried to get the turntable to move. No go; it didn't spin.

"The spring is busted," said Sasha. "The crank at the side won't catch."

Mario listened to the spring click. "It's slipped," he said. He took down the turntable and the old-fashioned trumpet, and handed them to Sasha. "Hold these."

With a screwdriver from his pocket, he began to take the victrola apart. He held the screws in his mouth and mumbled, "We could build a boat maybe. Hold it."

He tried to sound convincing.

"A motorboat would be best, but at least a sailboat. You can sail across the ocean in a sailboat. I'm sure of that. With the two of us we could even build a steamer. I can do anything. When I want to."

He spit the screws into the palm of his hand and caught the loose spring.

"Trouble is, most of the time I don't want to. Not when

it's the same old thing over and over forever. Like a squirrel in a cage."

He coiled the spring with precise motions. "That about the postcard—that's not a bad idea. To let them know where we are. On the way we might have to catch fish, though. To eat. One guy on the ocean drank the juice from fish when his water ran out. We'd have to have tons of water."

Fish fascinated Sasha. "There are rods and reels downstairs," he said excitedly. "And hooks."

"They're piddling."

Mario was out of breath from coiling the spring. It twisted up. "For the ocean you need hooks big enough for a cow. And an ax, too. For the sharks."

Suddenly he stopped and let go of the spring. It ripped across his fingers, but he didn't make a sound. He was listening.

A motorcycle was coming.

A dog barked.

Mario blew out the candle. Both boys stood stock-still in the darkness.

Sasha stammered, "I——" And then a panicky, "We have to get away."

The spring unwound with a whirr in the dark.

"Out back," Sasha said.

"How come?"

"They're looking for me. I left my notebook back there. In the truck. They're following the arrows."

"Quit the kidding."

"No, I wanted them to get you. On account of Slip, too."

The barking came closer.

"You're kidding me," Mario said again, but this time he believed it. He groped along the wall. "If you——" He was sweating. At last he found the door and the ladder to the attic.

"You fink! I should have kicked you silly right when I found you."

Spider webs stuck to his face as he crept up to the little window. He tore at them furiously.

Below him he saw a dog and some children pulling a cart with a shopping bag in it—probably beer and bread for lunch. The dog ran ahead to the lumberers and back in circles to the children. Then in an excess of joy, it started to roll in the grass, legs in the air and yelping like a puppy.

Mario sighed with relief.

Until he heard the roar of a motorcycle on the slope. It appeared on the little bridge—a police cycle with a white stripe. One policeman was driving and another was sitting on the back. The one on the back jumped off at the cabin farthest from them and walked around outside. He pushed the door and tried the shutters. Nobody.

"They'll be here in five minutes. Two cabins in between and then here." Always the sniveling next to him. Mario hissed, "You rat!"

Sasha turned white, his mouth dry, a lump in his throat.

"You little nothing of a rat."

The motorcycle rolled closer, then stopped again.

Time dragged on. A spider was sitting on the windowsill. It had eight feet. The back legs curled over the front ones like tentacles.

Mario stepped away from the window. Despite the dirt on the pane he could see the back of a man below, part of a front tire, and two hands being spit into and rubbed with a handkerchief. He heard the rapid breathing of the boy next to him. "I'm done for, no question," he thought.

"Why don't you yell?" Mario taunted. "One scream would do it." He felt the terror like a fist in his stomach. For a second perhaps he really wished it was all over. Everything.

Someone tried the door and the shutters downstairs. Then the footsteps stopped. "C'mon, let's go," said the one who was wiping his hands. "I think he probably caught a car on the highway."

The motorcycle started up, sounding tinny as it rattled over the slope in first gear. The policeman on the back bounced on the cushion and sang, "I wanna go home."

Mario turned to Sasha: "They don't care if you're missing. You're not worth a sneeze to anybody."

"To my folks."

"Nobody."

Sasha stepped back, waiting for Mario to beat him up again. He was afraid, but at the same time there were some things he knew, that the older boy could not talk him out of.

"They're bound to be worried about me—my father and my friends."

"Think so?"

Mario coiled the spring again. It seemed, for the time being at least, that the police were not going to find them. He
whistled. "Your friends would be the first to spit on you,"
he said. "I wouldn't count too much on them if I were you.
I bet I could knock you off right now, and nobody'd know
the difference. What's the matter, don't you believe that?"

"No."

"Okay, so don't then."

The spring clicked. The candlelight flickered over Sasha's
face. The turntable began to go around.

"Tell me one thing," Mario said. He collected the screws
and washers to bolt down the carriage. "When those two
were down there, all you had to do was yell. How come you
didn't?"

· E L V E S ·

They had eaten the last cracker. Outside the hill turned
gray and then it was night, as suddenly as though a window-
shade had been pulled down over the landscape. It was not
like the city, where the evening fades gradually into night.
It was a forest in autumn, readying for winter, without the
blue of blueberries or the warm odor of mushroom patches.
The stars might have been twinkling somewhere above, but
they were hidden in the mist.

There was only the inky night, full of crackling branches
and hushed footsteps in the grass.

Elves?

The candle blinked, and Sasha found it a fearful task, all of a sudden, to get to the spring with the bucket. He filled it and quickly ran back. Inside the cabin door he gulped thirstily, and the water landed in his stomach like a stone. Mario took even bigger gulps.

They had one night and one day behind them.

Mario had resolved to ditch Sasha the first chance he had.

And Sasha kept his eye on Mario, but he was no longer angry or afraid of him.

• MUSH •

Mario had been in the kitchen for a full hour, shaking out the contents of all the paper bags he could find. He returned with malt, two ounces of oatmeal, and three lumps of sugar. He poured the wine on top, stirred and tasted it.

"Have some. It's pretty good."

Sasha took a heaping spoonful. He shuddered as though he had swallowed castor oil. "It's sickening."

"You have to eat something."

Mario began elaborately spooning out the mush of malt, sugar, and wine.

"Look at me!"

But the mush stuck to his teeth, and he had to control his face. "It's sickening," he admitted, "but it's nourishing."

Some things that bothered Sasha seemed petty to Mario. Like hunger and dirty hands. Sasha didn't have a toothbrush with him and kept talking about it as if it were a problem.

64

Mario interrupted him: "Geronimo didn't brush his teeth either."

The eight o'clock news came on the radio. There had been a record in coal production. The beginning of the October holidays. Rivers were flooding somewhere, and bombs dropped on Africa. The official delegations had arrived at Ruzyne Airport.

"And he didn't have a lantern for the October parade, either."

"Who?"

"Geronimo."

Sasha felt something like homesickness whenever he remembered his friends. "You could sleep at our place," he said. "We could go to the parade together."

He imagined that one could make a mistake go away if he just confessed a hundred times in a notebook: *I'll never set a shed on fire again.*

· A PHOTOGRAPH ·

They were too hungry to sleep. Outside the half-open shutter it was dark and foggy. A little frost. The chill came in under the bed quilts. "I'll have to shut the window," said Mario, "before we freeze to death."

He knelt on the bed beside the boy. "You still feel lousy?"

"I've got a stomach ache." Sasha had mush up to his neck. "Think I don't?"

The bed hinges creaked and the candle sputtered to life.

Mario uncorked the wine and poured some for Sasha.

"It'll go away if you drink this."

"It's sour."

"Only at first."

The wine splashed. Sasha looked through the glass and watched Mario rummaging in his pockets.

"If you keep thinking about it, it'll never stop hurting," said Mario, shaking a handful of papers from his wallet. "Wanna see something?"

It was a photograph.

There were flags lining a racetrack and a few motorcycles tearing toward the finish. The figures of the drivers were so blurred they looked like smudges.

"The second one, that's me," Mario said. "In the dark helmet."

Sasha drank the wine without meaning to.

"Really?"

Sasha took the photograph and held it very carefully by the edges. He looked up admiringly at Mario and then back at the photograph. "Could I have it?" He pleaded, "Mister . . ."

"My name is Rudolf," said Mario. Sasha's admiration pleased him. He signed the photograph *From Rudy*. There was another one just like it in his wallet.

He said, "Remember—second place."

Sasha drank the wine. Now that he had the picture, it didn't taste so bitter. The room seemed to sway.

From a great distance he heard the voice of the racedriver whose name was Rudy.

"Sleep. Try to sleep for a while."

IIc knew that it was time to go, now, while Sasha was asleep. Morning was still a long way off, but tomorrow was Saturday. A lot of people would be coming to the cabins.

"I have a whole night and morning. I could be far away by then. I've got to make up my mind and do it, get it over with."

He wanted to leave, but he didn't. "I'll take him with me. If I leave him here, he'll die of fright."

But then, "I have to get rid of him sometime."

He didn't want to think about it. He tried to find reasons for keeping Sasha with him.

"Better to travel as two. They're looking for a boy alone. Alone, my chances of getting through would be much worse."

He knew that was a lie.

Because of the shed. And the shirtsleeve.

There were a million complications. "He'd slow me down. I'd have to let him sleep some, eat something."

But he went on lying in bed and looking into himself, and somewhere layers and layers before he was "Mario," he saw a small boy who looked something like Sasha. "Hey little guy, how are you?" he said. He had not faced that part of himself for a long time. Usually he pretended he had grown up wild, with wolves, or maybe barracuda. But the boy in him wasn't like that. "You wanna help me out of this mess, Rudy?"

Rudy put his wristwatch to his ear in disbelief. It was still ticking, and it said eleven. He had slept thirteen hours! There was the noise of a motorbike, the sound of footsteps on the porch, and the bed next to him was empty.

"I'm done for," he thought. "It's idiotic. I should have been out of here hours ago."

He didn't know yet what he would do. He went down the stairs like a cat, stopping every time the floorboards creaked. He saw the motorcycle through a gap in the logs, but it was not the police, it was a scooter. It was going off. A boy and girl, probably. He saw a girl's skirt flapping in the wind.

The downstairs room was empty. Rudy walked through to the lean-to, and crawled over some boards to the wooden privy.

He whispered cautiously, "Sasha?"

"I can't," came from within.

"Creep!"

"There isn't any paper in here."

Rudy found the schoolbag and shoved it under. "Tear some out of your notebook."

"No, I shouldn't."

For a second Rudy could have killed him. He got hold of himself. Some old newspapers were lying under the lumber. Yellowed headlines announced, BRITAIN'S QUEEN OPENS PAR-LIAMENT. RELIEF FOR THE AGED. He pushed them under the door.

"Hurry up!"

The door squeaked open at last.

"Did you sleep in there?"

"I've got a stomach ache."

Sasha came out, schoolbag in hand, looking seasick.

"Rudy . . ."

His eyes were wet. He wiped his nose with his elbow, completely confused. "I thought you were going to run away from me." Sniffle. "And I couldn't be any faster."

"Where's your coat?"

"I don't know."

They made a search of the main room. "It's here somewhere," Sasha whispered.

He crawled under a table and pushed the chairs around. "Rudy . . ."

"Hell, the hell with it." Rudy lifted an easy chair near the fireplace. "Oh, there's all the time in the world."

He found the coat on the staircase.

"Come on!"

Rudy collected his things. On the table was a cigarette holder in the shape of a woman. He started to put it in his pocket, but he saw Sasha looking at him. He left it on the table.

· I N T H E W O O D S ·

They scaled the hill, leaving the cabin farther and farther behind. Rudy stopped for a second as his foot hit a loose stone and sent it rolling down to the road. But there was no one to hear. Not even the lumbermen. A guitar twanged somewhere in the distance.

The pine needles smelled like resin. They put them in their mouths and ate them. Saliva seemed to dissolve some of the bitterness. It made a sort of tasteless gelatin that stuck to the roofs of their mouths, but the feeling of hunger went away. And the tiredness. It seemed as if they could walk forever, all the way to the sea.

"We forgot the fish hooks," Sasha said.

"Where?"

"At the cabin. The fish hooks." He walked in front of Rudy, pretending that he was at sea. "I have a rod and reel at home, but I never caught anything with it. I'd like to catch just one fish."

"Then what?"

"Nothing."

Sasha thought a minute, and laughed out loud. "Except maybe another one, bigger."

"And then another one, bigger than that?"

"Probably."

Rudy slowed down. Lying in the path ahead of him was an arrow made of pebbles. It pointed uphill in the direction they were walking. How or when Sasha could have made it, he didn't know, but he raked it out with the toe of his sandal.

"Maybe the fish don't want you to catch them. Maybe they'll pull you back down to the bottom with them."

They now walked alongside each other, off the edge of the path. Rudy was not going to let Sasha out of his sight.

The woods changed hour by hour. Cars drove along the road to the cabins. It was Saturday, which could be dangerous for them. All somebody had to do was walk into the cabin and find the melted candle, the dirty glasses, the beds.

They reached the top of the hill.

Below them, the little cabins looked glued to the rocky slope rising from the river valley. Smoke came from burning leaves. There were boys playing soccer with their fathers on a meadow. And at least ten paper kites in the sky. A train chugged along the towpath. They followed it with their eyes until it disappeared in a tunnel.

"I have three crowns," Sasha offered. "If you want——"

But Rudy was not listening. For a moment he observed a world to which he did not belong. Girls at the volleyball nets. Someone strumming a guitar by a campfire.

"He has an electric!"

"Keep going."

The branches of the forest closed behind them. They slid down the slope.

· GRASS ·

"Mountains of food," said Rudy. "I've got money somewhere. Once we get there . . ."

The sharp grass reached nearly to their waists. They seemed to disappear in it.

"When?"

"I don't know—but I know where we are now."

They had come out on the edge of the forest. Rudy bent down and tied the string on his sandal. The buckle was broken.

He picked a handful of mushrooms from a stump. They

looked like chanterelles, and the place was full of them.

"Not poison," he said offhand. "You can eat them. Raw or cooked, but cooked is best."

He spiked some of the mushrooms on a stick. "Better than moldy crackers, that's for sure," he told Sasha after lighting a small fire.

Then, "You're gonna get me mad with that sniffling of yours. Don't you have a handkerchief?"

"It's wet," Sasha said.

He went on sniffling and ate his mushrooms raw. He held his frozen hands over the fire. "My parents must be really worried, wondering what happened to me."

The mushrooms sputtered. Rudy turned the stick.

"We'll send them the first picture with a lion." He looked at the string on his sandal. "We'll have dough then. We'll be doing whatever we feel like. We'll buy first-class shoes and fish hooks and a first-class rifle. Okay by you?"

"I'd like to go home," Sasha said.

"Think I wouldn't?" said Rudy. He began to pull the mushrooms off the stick. "Think I wouldn't, you dummy, except that I don't even have a bed there any more. A week after they got me, someone else was sleeping in my bed."

"I didn't know that," Sasha said quietly. Suddenly he felt sorry for Rudy.

• PUDDLES •

"I've got a brother—that's all."

It was getting dark. The branches closed over their heads.

There were puddles on the path, and they had to go around them. The path narrowed.

"This is the long way," Rudy said. "Boy, the guys will really stare. Alice, too. It's almost two years since I saw her."

"Then what?"

Rudy remained silent for a while. Branches crackling, that was all.

"The dough and everything."

He changed the subject, feeling trapped by something he didn't want to think about. "We can buy frankfurters."

The path wound downhill.

Rudy heard a rustle and the scurrying of feet. And then a noise in the bushes behind him. There was a freshly drawn arrow in the mud. He erased it.

"Sasha!"

He ran in the direction of the noise, directly into the boy as he crawled out from the bushes.

"What are you doing in there? You're too little—you can't doublecross *me*!"

"My stomach hurts," said Sasha, not understanding. His hand went to his face. Too late—Rudy slapped him anyway.

"That'll stop it soon enough," he snapped. "Guaranteed." He pushed Sasha back on the path.

A few yards ahead, beyond the puddles, was another arrow made out of pebbles and pointing to a forked tree. A piece of paper was stuck in the bark of the tree.

"Look—somebody's laid out a treasure hunt!"

Sasha said nothing. He followed slowly. After being slapped for nothing, he meant to keep a distance. He heard Rudy trying to puzzle out the note.

"This is really dumb. *You're getting close.* Written back-ward."

Rudy kicked apart another arrow, made of twigs. "Candy, probably. Maybe chocolate," he said hopefully. He looked for more clues. "Their eyes are gonna pop if we find the treasure before they do."

He saw a piece of string tied to the branch of a fir tree. At the foot of the tree were five toy animals arranged in a row: a bear, a mouse, two owls, and a kangaroo.

It took him a minute to figure the riddle out.

He got it! The mouse was supposed to be a rat.

The answer was *brook*.

· T H E   T R E A S U R E ·

The last clue was spelled out in pine cones at the edge of the brook: the word *treasure*, written in Morse code.

Sasha stood on the bank with his hands in his pockets as Rudy poked in the water with a stick.

"It weighs a ton," he shouted. He had one leg knee-deep in the brook, but he didn't care. "It's in a tin box. To keep the water out."

Rudy maneuvered the box toward the bank.

Sasha was stumbling nearer, hopping from foot to foot.

"Why are you shaking like that?"

"I'm cold. And . . ." He had the runs and he wanted to go, but he didn't move. He was bursting with curiosity.

Rudy slid the box nearer. "A little bitter chocolate, that'll fix you up fine." He banged the lid off the box with a stone.

On top were badges. Underneath was something wrapped in newspaper. Pamphlets. *What Every Scout Should Know. How to make a turtle out of a nutshell. How to make a toothbrush from natural materials found in the forest. Begin by carefully fraying one end of a green stick . . .*

"Stick *them!*" shouted Rudy, throwing the pamphlets in the water and the badges after them.

But Sasha ran for the badges.

"I have this one . . . but I don't have this one." He followed slowly behind Rudy. "An Eagle. Here's a Star."

The shouts of children came from the forest. A whistle.

Sasha pinned a badge on his chest: "A Gagarin!"

Rudy said in a sharp voice, "Where's your schoolbag?"

Sasha looked from hand to hand, as if he wanted it to appear by magic. "I . . ." He tried to remember. "I don't know. Probably where we ate. I still had it then." He took a hesitant step away. "I'll go get it."

"Are you crazy?"

Rudy caught up with him and jerked him around. The voices of the children were quite close now. And the whistle.

"Do you want them to catch us?"

"My math is in there."

"Tough!" said Rudy, dragging Sasha through the bushes. Their feet slipped in the mud. "In an hour we've had it, if they find your schoolbag. If they bring the dogs with them. They've been looking for you like mad for two days, but near Prague."

He leapt into the brook up to his knees. "Quick, in here! Dogs go crazy in water."

Sasha did not understand, but followed Rudy into the brook anyway. Then he slipped on a stone and fell. "I can't——" He felt dizzy and a sharp pain in his right side— the same kind of pain as when you run, before you get a second wind, like a knife in the side.

"Rudy!" he cried. "I can't."

But nobody helped him up. There was only the water swirling around.

"I have to——"

• A CROSSROADS •

A motorcycle somewhere. Rudy stopped short. He heard the boy crawling toward him, panting. It was dusk. All that was visible was the stark outline of the slope. The sound of the motorcycle receded, then came closer.

"A Vespa," he guessed. "Fifteen hundred. I had just enough for a Vespa. If only . . ."

"I didn't do it on purpose," Sasha said. His teeth were chattering.

Rudy began to feel the cold, too. He reached into his pocket and took out a flask he had taken from the cabin. He un-screwed the top.

"What's the difference?" he said, leaving a gulp of rum for Sasha and walking ahead. "Anyhow, they'd have left me holding the bag. Just like last time."

"Who?"

"Never mind."

They had come to a fork in the road. A dog barked somewhere far away. A flare soared above the hill and burst high in the sky. It made a crack like the report of a starter.

Sasha said, "They're looking for us."

He saw Rudy's face in the flash of light. It was scared, like yesterday, but there was something different.

"If we just keep on standing here we'll freeze to death. There's a cabin right over this hill. We can make it if you don't louse us up. We can't blow it now. We'll have to separate and meet. We can't let them see us together."

"Why?"

"Not here. Later on, okay. If they should get you, you're alone, right?"

Sasha nodded. Then he changed his mind. It was almost dark. "Please, can't I come with you?"

"No."

"Okay." He trusted Rudy. "But whoever gets there first will wait for the other one, right?"

They walked on alone, each taking different routes through the trees. After a few steps Rudy stopped and looked at his watch.

"Five minutes, then I move on."

He could still hear sniffling above him on the slope. Dogs barking. "I threw him to them like a bone. If they've found the schoolbag, that is. I've got plenty of time now. Besides, nothing is going to happen to him."

Rudy returned slowly to the crossroads. Squeezing between some trees, he heard something move in the underbrush above him.

It was Sasha.

"I had to——" he said guiltily, pulling up his pants. "Again." He crawled down. "Anything happen?"

"I was just looking for you," Rudy said. He reached in his pocket. "Here. So you won't be afraid."

He took out the toy revolver.

Sasha's eyes lit up. "Oh, boy!"

He clicked it and the little flame shot up.

"Okay, up there then."

Sasha was shaking with chill but he did as he was told, clicking the gun as he climbed. He gave a low whistle.

Rudy answered but he stood where he was. For a second he was undecided, then the flame of the lighter disappeared in the dark, and he moved off down the slope—opposite the direction they had agreed on.

• FIRECRACKERS •

Rudy told himself, "He'll be home in two hours. As soon as they find him. If they find the schoolbag. He has better shoes than I do. And he has the revolver. It cost thirty crowns. I gave it to him for a present. That was real of me. I didn't have to give him anything. Now he has the revolver and the photograph—and better shoes than I do. No busted buckles."

He groped at branches in the dark.

His thoughts came in a jumble. "Car convoy. But I have money. Hot meatloaf, two crowns. Alice. Fifteen hundred crowns. Nope, shoes first."

He knelt down and tied the string on his sandal for the third time. The sandals were caked with mud, and he felt like chucking them. No good at all.

"I'll be there by morning."

Where?

He seemed to hear sniffling again, quite close.

"Sasha?"

But it was just the forest. Rudy stood up uncertainly and walked on. He zipped his jacket to the neck. This time he heard the sniffling a few feet away. And footsteps. When he stopped, they stopped too.

It was obvious. There was no point in saying he had lost his way again. "I told you to go the other way!"

Sasha did not reply. He just tried not to lose Rudy, tried to keep up. Now and then he lit the way with the revolver.

Rudy tripped over a log and said crossly, "You'd better blow your nose." He sucked the blood from a cut on his knuckle and spit it out. On the other side of the woods a fire rocket burst in the sky.

They didn't know whether the flares were on account of them, but high up the lights were bursting more and more often. And dogs barking.

"All because of you!"

Rudy tried to count the number of dogs. Four.

The ground was soaked in places. Rudy fell in up to his ankles, Sasha's wet face alongside him.

Other times Sasha lagged behind, walking in a stupor, licking his lips. All he wanted was to lie down in the grass and go to sleep. He remembered the tin can by the garage. The caps. "If they're still there. I have to keep going. For Slip."

He tried to focus on Rudy's back and hand. It was an enormous, swinging hand. Back and forth, back and forth. Forward. Backward. Then the world began to rock with geysers of light, and he fell down. He heard Rudy's voice way above him in the darkness.

"What's the matter with you?"

He tried to get to his feet. "I'm coming. Just a second. I'm thirsty."

He put his face in the brook. "I'm thirsty, I'm thirsty, I'm thirsty."

But there was no brook. Only the sting of pine needles. He was shaking all over. He watched the hand recede in the darkness, and shot at it with the revolver.

The rockets lit up like matches in the sky, in the treetops, one after another. It was getting warmer. Sasha's face was stinging. "Sit up straight," he told himself.

Then he realized that he was still holding the lit revolver. He blew out the flame. Darkness flew down at him from the branches. He was alone.

· BROKEN GLASS ·

Rudy slowed down and wiped the sweat and pine needles off his face. He was alone at last. Only silence behind him. He had come to the outskirts of the woods, which was full of rusty cans and trash.

Three yards ahead he saw a white kitchen stool without a back. Baby carriages without wheels. Rusty washbasins. Broken bottles.

He waded through the dump. "There's got to be a road out of here. How the devil do they get in?"

His sandals came loose again, and he was afraid of cutting his feet on the glass. But he kept walking, telling himself, "I feel great. I'm alone. I'll get out of it." And, "That dope. With his dopey shed."

The glass broke underfoot.

"That means luck."

He began to believe it. Beyond the dump he found a stream in the bushes and drank thirstily. The cool water ran down between his fingers, over his cheeks, and inside his jacket.

"That dope."

He straightened up, took a few wavering steps, and stopped. Suddenly he didn't feel like running at all. He listened to the sound of the wind in the branches. Thought he heard sniffling. Surprisingly, it made him glad.

"Sasha?"

But it was nothing, only a loose stone in the darkness. It rolled down the path. A fine drizzle began.

He went back and rummaged in the dump. Raindrops were plopping into the puddles. He tried to retrace his steps.

"Sasha?"

Coming out of the darkness he saw a group of trees with white marks on them. Chalk. They had been condemned because they were dead.

"Alexander!"

A light flickered in the darkness. Sasha lay on the ground, sniffling and staring at the flame from the revolver. He hardly noticed as Rudy reached him and bent down with a half-full can of water. Rudy held the can to Sasha's lips as he drank. "Don't cut yourself."

Dogs were barking somewhere, but it didn't matter any more. He helped Sasha to his feet.

"Hold on to me. We're going home."

He looked for the path. "Watch out for the branches."

Sasha murmured weakly, "We have a couch in the living-room. You can sleep on it."

He had probably been thinking that all this time. It was nonsense, Rudy knew it was nonsense, but he said, "Okay. Sure."

He was almost carrying Sasha. They were still in the forest, but below them Rudy could see lights flitting by on the road and hear the rumble of trucks. Then the trees thinned again, and suddenly it was only ten yards to the highway.

Fireworks soared up over the outskirts of a nearby town. Luminous little trees and sparks and stars shone through the rain. Rudy heard the voices of children. Kids on bikes streamed along the highway, probably coming from the October parade—he could tell from the lanterns on the handlebars. Again darkness.

Then out of the night came the lights of an approaching truck. Rudy crossed the ditch and waved. Brakes screeched. The headlights came to a stop next to him. An old man bringing his ducks to market.

"Nice mess you've made of yourselves," the porter said as Rudy led Sasha into the emergency room of the hospital. Alone now, Rudy wiped up the mud he had tracked over the linoleum. The rush of a shower and the clink of hypodermic needles. He knew they would be here any minute now, coming to get him, but he didn't care—the important thing was that he had come back and didn't have to keep running forever.

"Just want to sleep."

He washed his hands and face in the corner of the hall for five minutes. Dried mud fell from his pants cuffs onto the floor. He kept picking it up and carrying it across the corridor to the trashbasket. So it was quite by chance that he saw Sasha, coming from the shower, sailing through the air on the arms of a nurse, wrapped up in a towel and looking warm and clean.

"I didn't yell a bit," he called proudly, "even when they stuck me with needles. Are you going to wait for me? They say they're coming for us in a car."

Rudy looked out the window into the rain. A car with a white stripe pulled up in the parking lot. Three men in uniform got out.

He tried to smile at Sasha just as the door closed behind him.

Room number twenty-two.

He thought of the couch with nobody sleeping on it.

Footsteps were climbing up the stairs. And voices.

"Crazy kids."

Then another policeman laughed. "And Frank's still combing the woods."

"Let's get a beer."

Rudy zipped up his jacket and stuck his hands in his pockets to hide his fear. He began to walk slowly down the corridor in the direction of the approaching uniforms. The policemen passed him, and he listened as their footsteps continued on down the corridor. One of them stopped, turned, and came back toward him.

"Where is he?"

"In here," called a nurse.

The door clicked.

Rudy stood where he was. Nobody was arresting him. "What about me?" he said as the policeman walked off. "What about me?"

OTA HOFMAN, born in 1928, is an avant-garde Czech filmmaker who now lives in Prague. He has written a number of film scripts for and about children. Several of his original screenplays have been published in book form, including *Rabbits in High Grass, Tale of the Old Streetcar,* and *Clown Ferdinand and the Rocket. Escape* is the first book by Mr. Hofman to appear in English.

ALAN E. COBER is a well-known illustrator of books for children. Among his many honors are the Gold Medal for 1969 from the Society of Illustrators and the Artists Guild "Artist of the Year" award for 1965. *Mr. Corbett's Ghost,* which he illustrated for Pantheon Books in 1968, was cited by *The New York Times* as one of the Ten Best Illustrated Books of that year. Mr. Cober and his wife Ellen live with their two children in a 160-year old house in Ossining, New York. *Escape* is his fourth book for Knopf.

Text set in Baskerville
Composed by Maryland Linotype Composition Co., Baltimore, Maryland
Printed by Halliday Lithograph Corp., Hanover, Massachusetts
Bound by Economy Bookbinding Corp., Kearny, New Jersey
Typography by Atha Tehon